This igloo book belongs to:

....

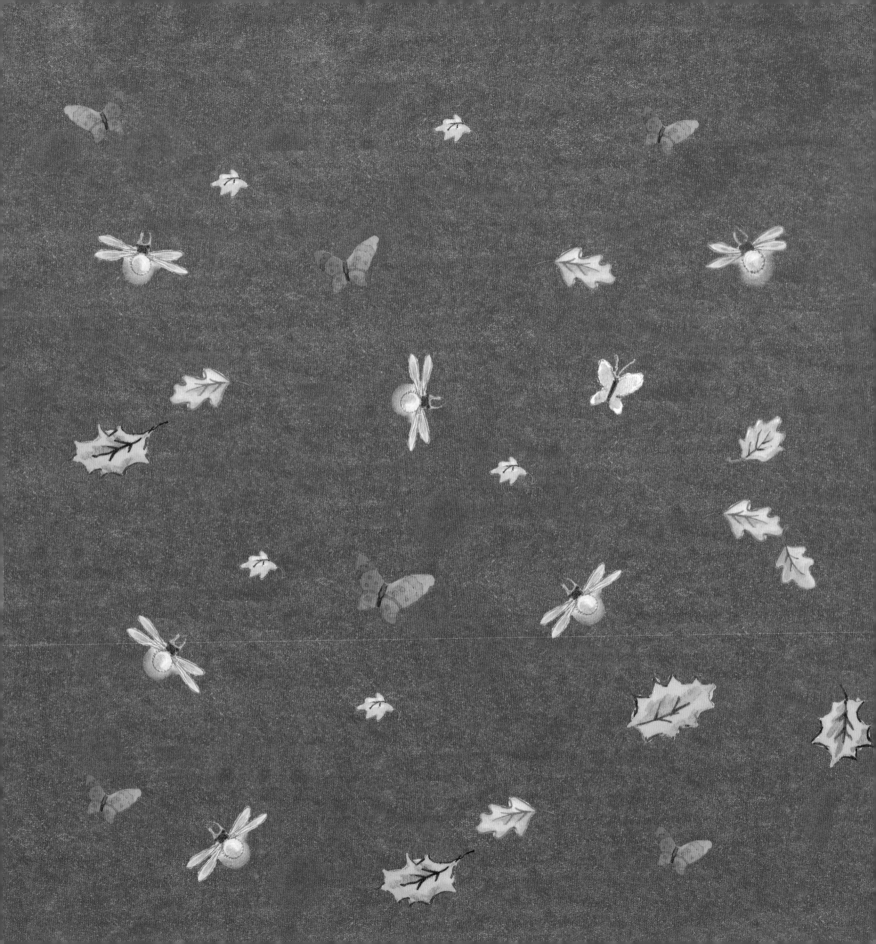

igloobooks

Published in 2014
by Igloo Books Ltd
Cottage Farm
Sywell
NN6 0BJ
www.igloobooks.com

HUN001 0414
8 10 12 11 9
ISBN: 978-0-85780-434-1

Printed and manufactured in China

Bedtime, Little Bear

igloobooks

Late one afternoon, Little Bear was balancing
on an old log. It was a good game.

"Time for bed, Little Bear!" called Mother Bear.
"It's getting late!"

Little Bear stopped balancing for a moment… and fell off!
He didn't feel a bit sleepy.

"I don't think that can have been Mother Bear calling me,"
he said to himself. "It must have been the trickling stream."

A few minutes later, Little Bear found some lovely leaves to play in. His friend, Mouse, passed by.

"Little Bear," called Mouse, "I think I heard Mother Bear calling you."

Little Bear poked out his head. He didn't want to
stop playing. He was having so much fun!

"I don't think that can have been Mouse's squeaky voice,"
he said to himself. "It must have been the rustling leaves."

When Little Bear finished playing,
he noticed that the sky was as red and gold as
the fallen leaves he had been playing in.

He climbed a tree to get a better view.

High in the branches, his friend Squirrel
was scampering past.

"Little Bear!" called Squirrel. "Didn't I hear Mother
Bear and Mouse calling to you?"

Little Bear hugged the trunk. "That wasn't Squirrel
calling," he said to himself. "It must have been the
breeze swishing through the trees."

Little Bear watched as the sun slipped behind the hill. Then he climbed down to the bottom of the tree.

Shadows were deepening all around him.
"It's time to go home," said Little Bear.

As Little Bear trudged through the trees,
the moon rose up into the sky and
all the twinkling stars came out.

"It's almost as light as day," said Little Bear. But somehow things looked different at night and scary, too. Little Bear wasn't sure which way to go.

Now, Little Bear thought that maybe someone *had* been calling him. He wished that he had answered. What if he could never find his way home?

Just then, he heard a tiny sound… "Little Bear!"

Little Bear listened harder.

"Little Bear! Little Bear! Little Bear!"

"That's not the trickling stream," said Little Bear.
"And it's not rustling leaves, or the breeze in the trees.
It sounds like Mother Bear!"

And it was! Little Bear ran right into
Mother Bear's warm, furry arms.

Mouse and Squirrel, who had been helping
Mother Bear search for Little Bear,
did a little dance of delight.

Little Bear felt very sleepy now, so Mother Bear carried him home to his snuggly bed.

"Good night, Little Bear," said Mother Bear softly.

"Good night, Little Bear!" called Mouse
from his comfy bed.
"Good night, Little Bear," said Squirrel
from his treetop nest.

It was peaceful in the woodland
and all that could be heard
was the trickling stream…
… and the rustling leaves…
… and the breeze in the trees.
And a little bear snoring, softly.

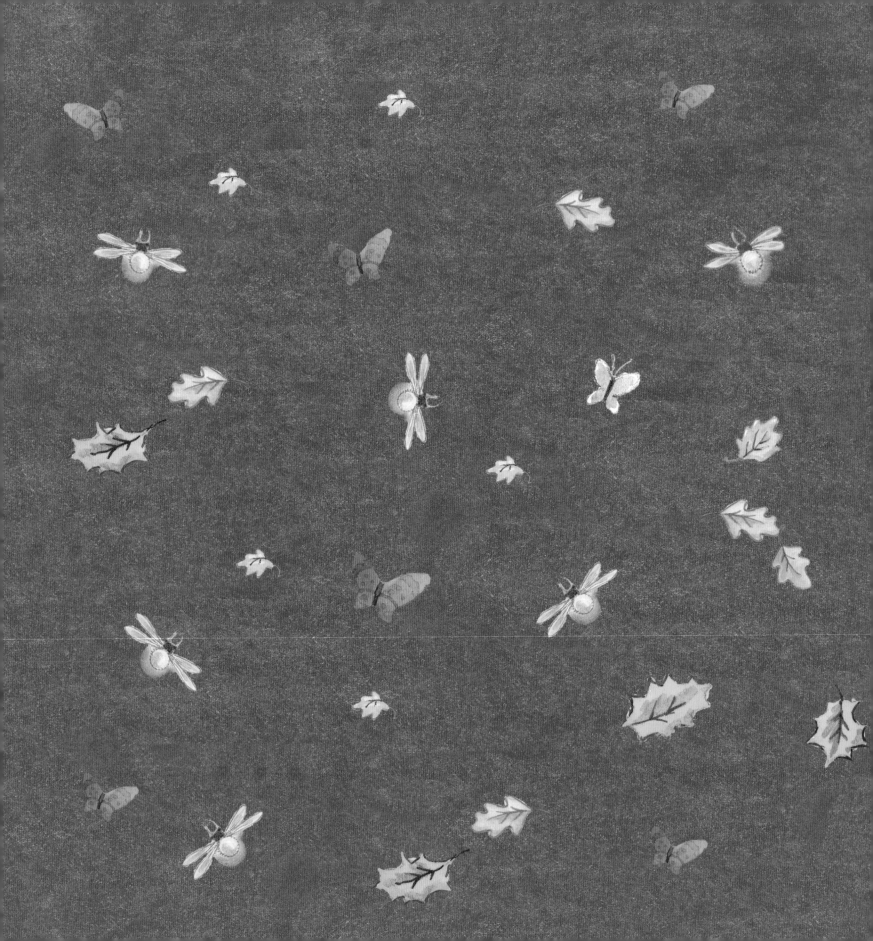